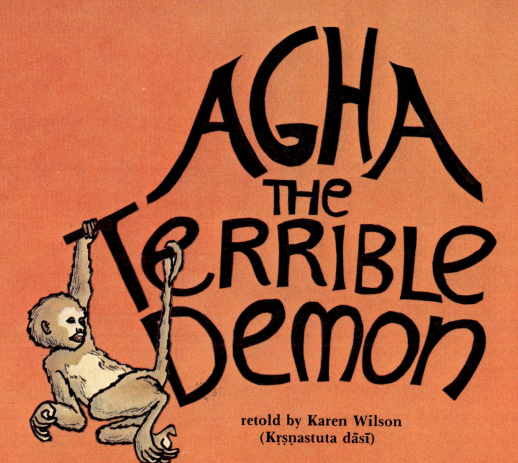

AGHA THE TERRIBLE DEMON

retold by Karen Wilson
(Kṛṣṇastuta dāsī)

illustrated by
Marie Thérèse Dubois

graphic design by
Jan Steward

edited by
Joshua Greene
(Yogeśvara dāsa)

Agha the Terrible Demon **is based on the** *Bhāgavata-Purāṇa,* **Tenth Canto, available in English under the title** *Kṛṣṇa, The Supreme Personality of Godhead* **(© 1970 by the Bhaktivedanta Book Trust), translated from the original Sanskrit by His Divine Grace A. C. Bhaktivedanta Swami Prabhupāda, Founder-Ācārya of the International Society for Krishna Consciousness.**

FIRST PUBLISHED IN THE UNITED STATES IN 1977 BY
BALA BOOKS, 340 West 55th Street,
New York, N. Y. 10019

© 1977 BY BALA BOOKS

Library of Congress Cataloging in Publication Data

Kṛṣṇastuta dāsī.
   Agha the Terrible Demon.

   "Based on the *Bhāgavata-Purāṇa,* Tenth Canto."
   SUMMARY: Krishna saves His friends, the cowherd boys,
from a giant serpent whose corpse is then turned into
a playground.
   1. Krishna—Juvenile literature. [1. Krishna.
2. Mythology, Hindu] I. Bhaktivedanta Swami, A. C.,
1896-   II. Dubois, Marie Thérèse. III. Purāṇas.
Bhāgavata-Purāṇa. Canto 10. English. IV. Title.
BL1220.K77 1977   [294.5]   [E]   77-10642
ISBN 0-89213-007-5

Long, long ago,
in a place we now call India,
Krishna sported with His cowherd boyfriends,
just like an ordinary child...

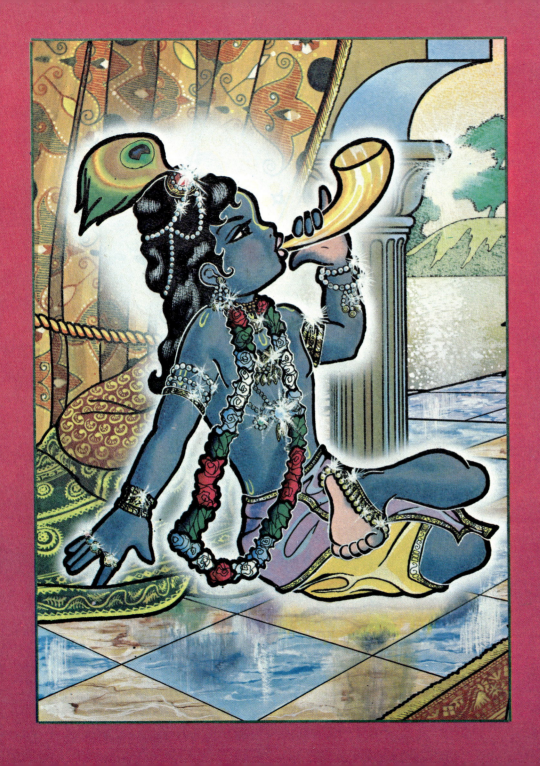

Every morning in the village of Vrindaban, Krishna blew His buffalo horn to gather all His friends together.

There were thousands of cowherd boys who cared for thousands of calves. Each boy had a stick, flute, horn and lunch bag. Each wore pearls, gems and gold ornaments.

Each decorated himself with flowers, leaves, twigs, peacock feathers and red clay found here and there in the forest. Always happy, the boys played many games. Sometimes Krishna went on alone to view the beauty of the forest. The boys behind Him tried to catch up and be the first to touch Him. One would cry out, "I will run and catch Him!" Another would cry, "Oh no you won't! I'll get to Krishna first!"

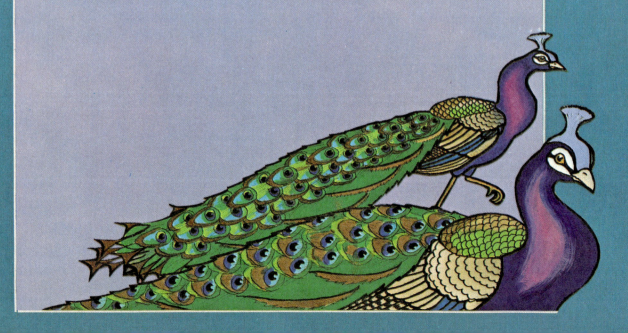

Sometimes one boy stole another boy's lunch and passed it to a third. When the boy whose lunch was stolen found out, he tried to take it back. But they continued to pass it from boy to boy.

Some of the boys caught the tails of the young monkeys hanging in the trees. Others climbed up the trees with them, making faces at them or jumping from branch to branch.

Some of them played their flutes or blew their bugles made of buffalo horn. Some sang with the music of the black bees.

Some followed the swans, and some ran after the shadows of the birds.

Some of the boys sat with the cranes, while others danced with the peacocks. Some imitated the cuckoo—"Cookoo! Cookoo!"

COOKOO
COOKOO
COOKOO
COOKO
O COO
KOO

Some splashed in the water and imitated the frogs. Some laughed at the shadows and cursed the echoes they made in the wells. Thus they spent their days in the forest of Vrindaban.

One day, Krishna and His friends were enjoying themselves in the forest.

A mighty and terrible demon named Agha watched them. He hated to see them having so much fun. He decided to kill Krishna and all His friends. This demon was so terrible that even the residents of heaven were afraid of him. As he watched, he thought, "This Krishna is the boy who killed my demon sister, Putana, and my demon brother, Baka! Now I'll kill His friends and calves. With the children dead, all the people of Vrindaban will die of grief!"

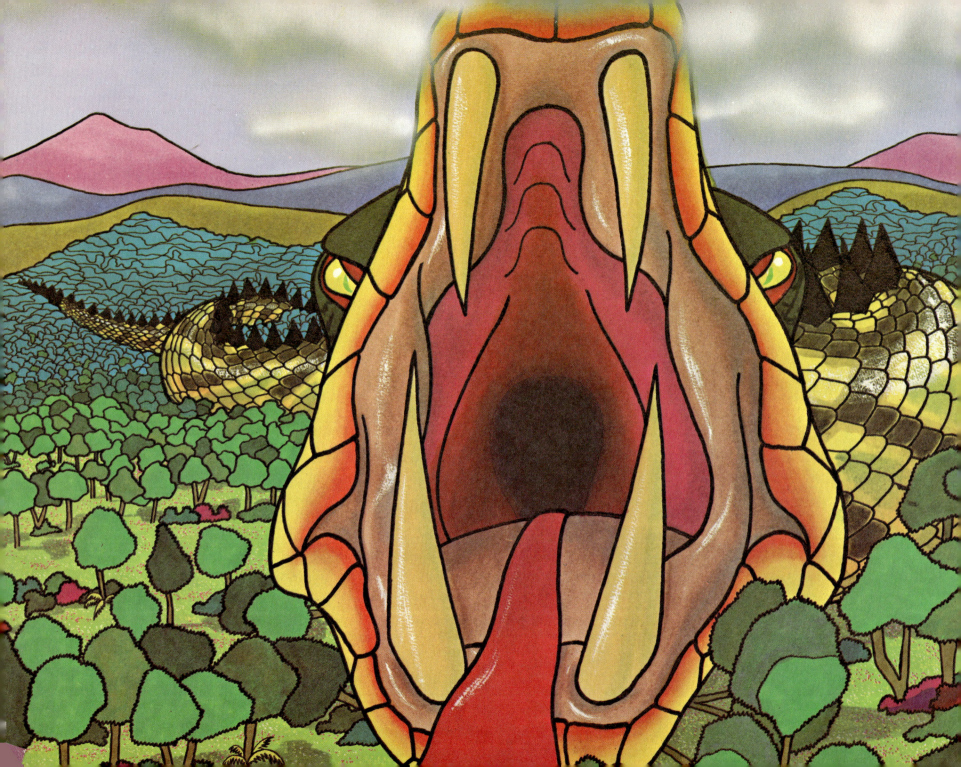

Then the terrible demon Agha grew longer and longer until he was eight miles long. He stretched his mouth open wider and wider until it was as wide as a mountain cave. His sharp teeth appeared like peaks on that mountain, and his hot tongue appeared like a broad road. His eyes blazed fire. Agha decided to swallow Krishna and the boys all at once. So he sat on the path and waited.

When the boys first saw the demon, they thought he was a statue. They began to talk among themselves.

"What is this?" said one boy. "It appears to be a huge animal. He looks like he wants to swallow us all!"

"Just see!" said another. "Isn't it a big snake that has opened his mouth wide just to eat us?"

"His breath is a fierce hot wind," said a third boy, "and the fishy bad smell from his mouth is the smell of his intestines. But he cannot swallow us all at once. Even if he did, Krishna would kill him."

And so, unafraid, they marched right into the mouth of the demon.

Agha waited for Krishna.

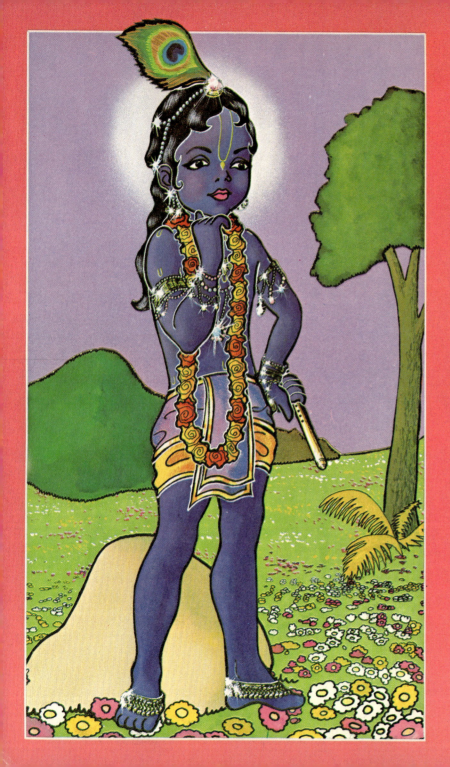

For a moment, Krishna felt very sad. His friends were lying in the belly of a great serpent! "How will I save them?" He wondered. Then Krishna entered Agha's mouth.

All the demigods hiding in the clouds were afraid. They cried out,

"Alas! Alas!"

Once inside the demon's throat, Krishna grew bigger and bigger. Agha choked, thrashed about, and his big eyes moved violently. His life-air burst from a hole in the top of his head and waited in the sky. It was like a dazzling light that spread everywhere.

Inside Agha's belly, Krishna found His friends unconscious. With His mystic glance, He brought them all to life. Then they marched right out of the demon's mouth.

Suddenly, Agha's glittering spirit soul merged into the body of Krishna. The demigods became overwhelmed with joy. They showered flowers on Krishna. They danced and beat drums and sang songs. "Jaya! Jaya! All glories to Krishna!"

The gigantic, fierce mouth of the demon stayed open for many days. Slowly his body dried up.

So they used it for a playground.

Thus ends the story of Krishna
and the demon Agha.
This is only one of Krishna's adventures—
so wonderful to tell
that they are worth telling another time,
in another book.